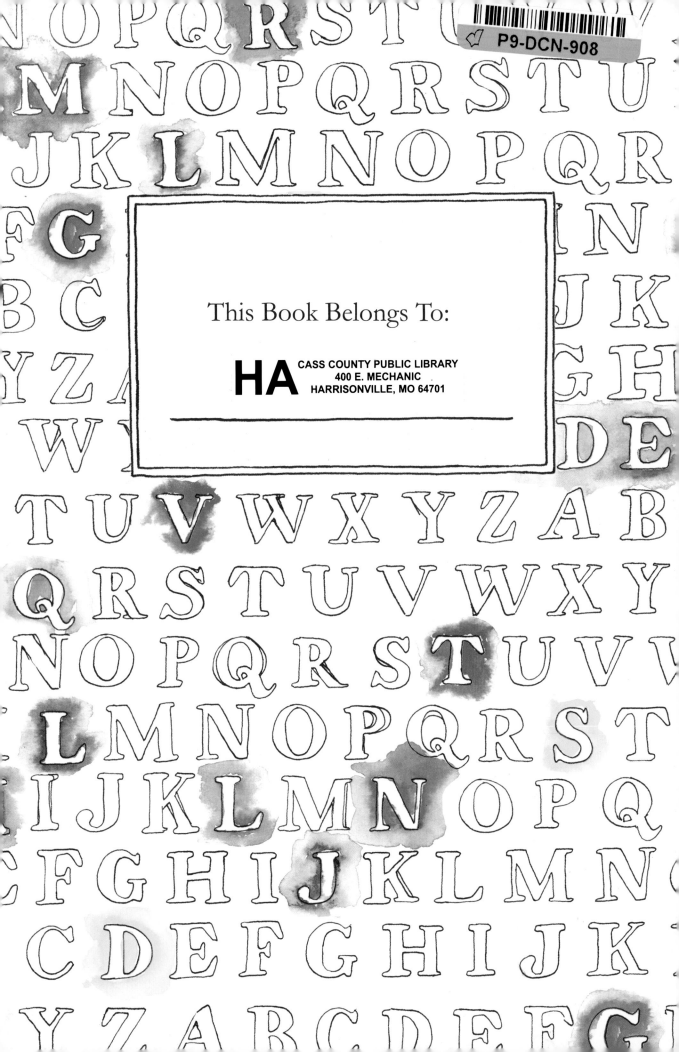

This Book Belongs To:

For the inner child
—K.K.

Copyright © 2016 by Kim Krans

All rights reserved. Published in the United States by Random House
Children's Books, a division of Penguin Random House LLC, New York.

Random House and the colophon are registered trademarks
of Penguin Random House LLC.

Visit us on the Web! randomhousekids.com

Educators and librarians, for a variety of teaching tools,
visit us at RHTeachersLibrarians.com

Library of Congress Cataloging-in-Publication Data
Krans, Kim, author, illustrator.
ABC dream / by Kim Krans. — First edition.
pages cm
Summary: Drawings of creatures and natural wonders introduce the letters of the alphabet.
ISBN 978-0-553-53929-5 (trade) — ISBN 978-0-553-53930-1 (lib. bdg.) — ISBN 978-0-553-53931-8 (ebook)
[1. Alphabet.] I. Title.
PZ7.1.K7Ab 2016 [E]—dc23 2015008746

MANUFACTURED IN CHINA

10 9 8 7 6 5 4 3 2 1

First Edition

ABC
DREAM

KIM KRANS

Random House 🏠 New York

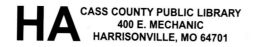

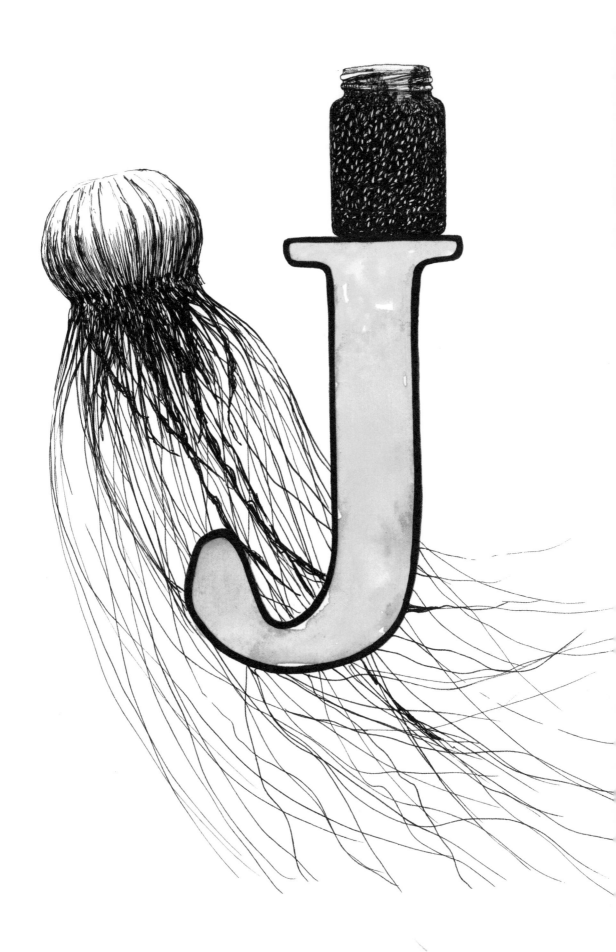

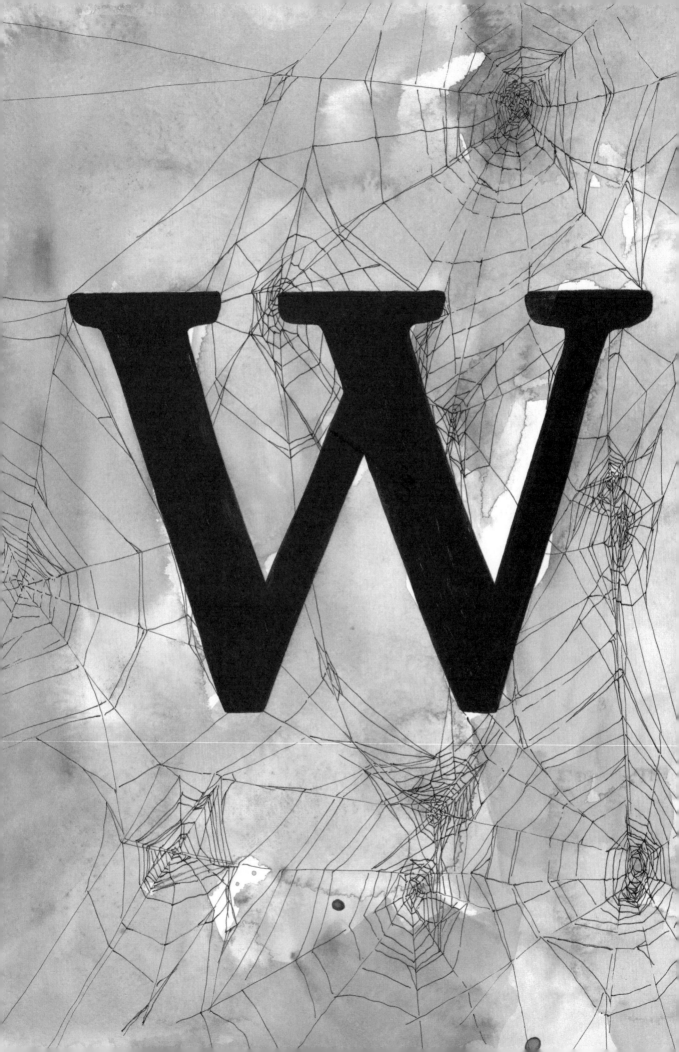

A
ANTS
APPLES
ARGYLE
ARROWS

B
BLUE
BOW
BRAID
BRANCHES
BRICKS
BUTTERFLY

C
CHERRY
CHICKEN
CHOCOLATE
CORNERS
CRUMBS
CUPCAKE

D
DALMATIAN
DANDELIONS
DIAMONDS
DOG
DRAGONFLY

E
EARTH
EGG
EUROPE

F
FEATHERS
FERNS
FIREFLIES
FISH
FLYING
FOX

G
GOOSE
GRASS
GRASSHOPPERS

H
HAT
HEARTS
HEDGEHOG
HINGES

I
ICE CREAM
IRIS

J
JAM
JAR
JELLYFISH

K
KEY
KITTENS

L
LACE
LAMB
LEANING
LEAVES
LINE
LION
LYING DOWN

M
MIRROR
MOON
MOUNTAINS
MOUSE

N
NEST
NIGHT

O
OCTAGON
OLD
OWL

P
PALM TREE
PANDA
PLAID
PUZZLE

Q
QUAIL
QUARTERS
QUEEN
QUILT

R
RAIN
RED
REFLECTION
RING
ROBIN
ROPE
ROSE

S
SAND
SEASHELLS
SHINE
SNAIL
SPIDER
STARS
STRAWBERRY
SUN

T
TIGERS
TIRED
TREE
TRUNK
TWO

U
UNICORN
UPSIDE-DOWN

V
VINES
VIOLIN

W
WASPS
WATERMELON
WEBS

X
X-RAY

Y
YARN

Z
ZEBRA
ZIGZAGS
ZINNIAS